La Brea Tar Pits
Pozos de La Brea

WRITTEN AND ILLUSTRATED BY JOSE CABRERA
INSPIRED AND ASSISTED BY CHIARA & NAOMI TUCKER CABRERA

A bilingual book

Este libro pertenece a: ______________________________

Visit **upandover.xyz** to order more books

cover design: Jose Cabrera

"Ardilla wake up, today is the day we go see the dinosaurs," said Bunny.

"Ardilla despierta, hoy es el día que vamos a ver a los dinosaurios," dijo Bunny.

"Bunny, there were no dinosaurs during the ice age. They weren't equipped for the cold," said Ardilla.

"Bunny, no hubo dinosaurios durante la era de hielo. No estaban equipados para el frío," dijo Ardilla.

"Animals like this family of mammoths walked on earth during the Pleistocene era about 40,000 years ago," explained Ardilla.

"Animales como esta familia de mamuts caminaron sobre la tierra durante la era del Pleistoceno hace unos 40,000 años," explicó Ardilla.

"And the reason they call this place the tar pits is because a lot of the animals got stuck and eventually became extinct," continued Ardilla.

"Y la razón por la que llaman a este lugar pozos de brea es porque muchos de los animales se quedaron atrapados y finalmente se extinguieron," continuó Ardilla.

"Bunny, be careful where you step or you can get stuck just like these mammoths!" called out Ardilla.

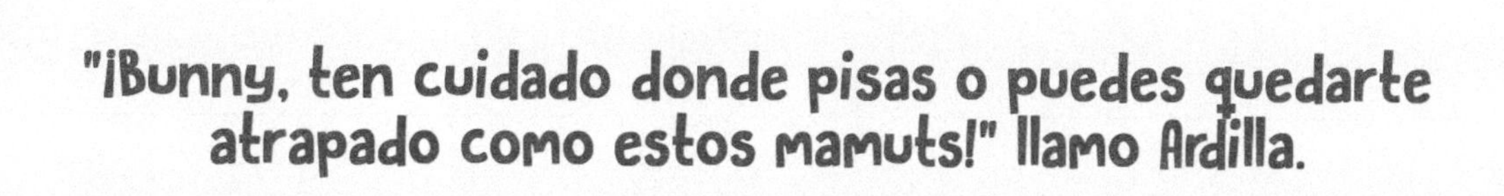

HH

¡ESTOY ATASCADO!

"Hold ... on ... one ... second!" grunted Bunny.

"¡Espera ... un ... segundo!" gruñó Bunny.

"Don't worry amigos, I'll get you out!" shouted Chango.

¡No se preocupen amigos, los sacaré!" gritó Chango,

NNNNNNN

SMACK

"Did I mention that when animals got stuck they became easy dinner for sabertooth cats," trembled Ardilla.

"¿Mencioné cuando los animales se atascaron se convirtieron en una cena fácil para los gatos de dientes de sable," tembló Ardilla.

"You guys seem to be in a sticky situation!" said Greenie.

"¡Ustedes parecen estar en una situación pegajosa!" dijo Greenie.

GRRRRRRRRRRRRRR

FWOP!

"Hey guys! I see that you're in a pickle. I'll use a few olives to get you out," said Birdie.

¡Hola chicos! Veo que están en apuros. Usaré unas aceitunas para sacarlos," dijo Birdie.

GET
HELP!
¡BUSCA AYUDA!

OLIVE
OIL
ACEITE
DE OLIVA

"Sorry that we doubted you Birdie!" said Bunny.

"¡Lamento que te hayamos dudado Birdie!" dijo Bunny.

Made in the USA
Columbia, SC
19 June 2024

37269656R00015